The Keeper of the Lost

King of the Castle

Table of Contents

CHAPTER ONE

Daven's house, same evening

"Rupert, we have a problem. Hank agreed to stay away from the office for a few days."

"But…wait, that's what we asked him to do!"

Daven grunted. "Now we can't keep an eye on what he's doing. He's given up already, thinks he's lost this battle. He's going to focus on bringing Harmon down instead of absolving himself."

"Wait. I'm confused. Back up, Dav, you're freaking me out."

"Sorry. We talked for about two hours just now. He's going to recall his double agents, get all the dirt he can on Harmon, and take him down with him. Those were his words, not mine. He seems to be uninterested in trying to find a trail back to Colbert anymore. Told us to keep trying, but there was no point. He's convinced Colbert can't get caught."

Rupert's hair stood up on the back of his neck. "Oh, fuck. This is not good."

"It gets worse. He wants to do a press conference tomorrow at four o'clock. Not a media statement, mind you, but a full-on press conference. I think he's finally lost his mind, Rupe."

"Shit, well...he's the boss. I'll start preparing. In the meantime, it's your job to talk him out of it. I'm not going to get caught in a lurch if you can't succeed."

"Agreed. That would only make things worse. Wish me luck."

Seditionist HQ, 4pm

Daven was not successful in talking Hank down, and now he and Rupert silently leaned up against the back wall of the press room and watched their boss with a level of fear and awe they had never quite felt before. First off was Hank's media statement.

"Thank you all for coming," he stated calmly, and cheerfully. "As usual, I will start this off by reading our official media statement regarding the recent allegations against me and our organization in general:

The Seditionists are aware of the numerous allegations made Friday and Saturday against Hank Bancroft, leader of the party. Only one of the allegations are true: we do in fact utilize a small number of informants within the Urbanes organization. This practice is not, and has never been, illegal. Their work is limited to passive monitoring for illegal activity and reporting on the general morale of the party's employees and its constituents. Their purpose has never been to sabotage operations or release unauthorized information, and they are not paid for their services. However, in an abundance of caution, we have made the decision to recall all such persons back to Los Angeles effective immediately, and will not engage in this practice in the future."

There was a collective, excitable gasp from all around the newsroom. Daven let out the long breath he'd been holding, and Rupert fidgeted with his tie for the hundredth time.

All other allegations are categorically false and will be proven as such in very short order. Mr. Bancroft has personally made the decision to step down as leader of the Seditionists while these investigations are ongoing, in order to prevent situations at the office that may create tension or result in conflicts of interest. Daven Johansson, Chief Strategist, will lead the party until further notice. The investigation itself will be conducted primarily by Rupert Aster and Taylor Bowen, with the gracious assistance of an FBI auditor.

Hank set the statement down and hit the green button on his podium. "I have ten minutes for questions."

Urbanes HQ - Denver

"My god. Balls of steel, that man. No matter how much I hate him, got to say it." Harmon whistled low and took another handful of chocolate covered almonds from the jar on Colbert's desk.

Umber shook his head, but didn't avert his eyes from the television. "For a smart man, he's not very smart sometimes. Putting his entire accounting staff on leave? Jesus Christ."

Colbert leaned forward. "Shhh, I think this is the last question. Bet you anything Hailey's going to get it."

Seditionist HQ

"Yes, number 27."

Hailey stood up, looking as smug as usual. "Mr. Bancroft, do you think these charges are just a string of easily explainable coincidences, or do you believe you're being framed?"

Daven and Rupe simultaneously tensed up. Again. They absolutely hated when Hank went for a free-for-all on questions like this, especially against Hailey.

Hank smiled. "Ms. Hendricks, I don't believe in coincidences. Next question, please?"

Daven glanced at his friend, who was sweating bullets. "He's doing pretty good, actually. Holding his own."

"Wish I could say the same for me," Rupert grumbled. "I'm one more question away from wetting my pants."

Hank punched the green button again. "Yes? Mr. Lowly."

Urbanes HQ - Denver

Colbert held his breath and tried not to draw attention to his sudden angst. Mark Lowly was one of the photographers Yannick paid off.

"Mr. Bancroft, it's well known that you offered to bribe photographers not to take pictures of your sons. You admitted as much, and were publicly censured for it. How is it that you now claim you made no such payments? Is such a statement supportable?"

"As I already said, Mr. Lowly, these payments were unauthorized. We're investigating them."

At this, Hank looked right into the Denver station's camera and smirked. It seemed to Colbert that the man was looking straight at him. Mocking him. Daring him.

"Wait, I don't get it," said Harmon slowly. "Who would be doing this to him? *We're* not. I mean...doesn't this seem incredibly strange? I know he has a lot of enemies, but if he's right, this is a pretty sophisticated operation."

Umber, who was secretly a huge fan of Hank's chutzpah but would never admit it to these particular men, laughed a little nervously. "Well, as long as he doesn't pin it on us, I don't care. Maybe one of his agents went rogue. More likely, he's guilty as hell. He's bribed people before, for god's sake. Almost got jailed for it a few times."

"Years ago," Harmon scoffed.

"Nobody's doing anything. He's guilty as hell, boss," said Colbert, as calmly as he could manage. Bancroft had no chance.

Until he did something totally unexpected, that is.

Hank cleared his throat. "I'm sorry, we've run out of time for questions. I want to strongly encourage the six photographers who allegedly received these payments from me to please call the FBI with information as to how, when, and where they received the money. Whether their answer implicates me or someone else, it's incredibly important that this information be made known as soon as possible in order to allow us to complete the investigation. If you do not call on your own accord, it is highly likely you will be subpoenaed to travel to Philadelphia to give testimony once my trial begins. Here is the number FBI's tip hotline. Oh, and forgive me for neglecting to mention that we even know where the cashier's checks were purchased, and we're very close to obtaining video of the person who bought them. We are hoping to link that person to the person who made the false payments. Possibly it is the same man or woman. Thank you for your time, and have a nice evening."

Oh, holy fuck... Colbert said to himself as he saw his entire future crashing down around him. If Yannick was identified, Harmon would see through the entire charade in a heartbeat. It was time to think fast.

"Boss, I think you ought to pull the trigger with that tape, now. Shoot this thing down before it grows wings and the public starts supporting him and saying we're framing him."

Harmon nodded. "I was thinking the same. He was pretty convincing, huh?"

Umber looked at the floor. "He's got *me* convinced we're framing him, for god's sake. I hate to admit it, but Colbert's right. We need to get the jump on him now."

"Agreed. Alright. We have to protect ourselves..and our party, more importantly. Let's do it. I'm going back to my office."

Seditionist HQ

Hank's office

Daven immediately busied himself making an espresso while Hank began packing up his things and prepared to go home for a while. *Hopefully not forever*, he mused.

Rupe was the first to speak. "Hank...I have to say, I'm incredibly impressed with how well you handled yourself. I'm sorry I ever fought with you about this press conference in the first place."

"It's alright, Rupe. You weren't wrong."

"What you said about the FBI subpoenaing the photographers, though. Was that true? I mean, we don't even know who they are, unless you know something we don't."

Hank grimaced. "Yeah, about that. I sort of made it up on the spot. I'm going to have hell to pay for that when Stewart hears about it, if he hasn't already-"

Hank's phone rang, and it was Stewart. "Speak of the devil. I'm going to put him on speaker so don't say anything, okay?"

The men nodded, and Hank answered the phone.

"Hank Bancroft."

"Hi, Hank. Stewart. Just watched your press conference."

Hank closed his eyes and took a deep breath. "I'm completely prepared for you to rip me a new one. Go ahead, I deserve it."

There was a brief pause. "You mean over the subpoena thing? No. I thought it was quite clever. Hell, if it leads to tips I can use, all the better for it. I was calling for something else. Did you receive the questionnaire packet yet? FedEx said it was delivered at 10:30am."

"Yes, I did."

"Good. The other thing is that I have some potentially upsetting news, Hank. Harmon has indicated he wishes to meet with me tomorrow. He's flying out tonight on a red-eye. I didn't want you to hear it on the news first."

Oh, shit. "Okay. Thanks for letting me know. What does that mean for me, exactly?"

Stewart replied, "He hasn't actually told me, but I think you know what it could mean."

"Yeah." There was only one reason Harmon would ever willingly meet with Stewart.

"You should prepare to meet with me to discuss this. If he...god, I hate to tell you this over the phone in this manner. But if he does have enough evidence for us to press criminal charges-"

"You'll have to arrest me." Hank swallowed hard. "When?"

"Assuming that's the reason he's coming, Thursday. Possibly Friday. You really should make finishing that questionnaire a priority."

Hank's throat was dry, and he had to swallow a few times to reply. "Make it Monday. I need one more weekend with my kids."

"Just a second."

Stewart put him on hold; he didn't dare look at Daven or Rupert in the meantime.

"Hank," said Rupe softly.

"Shhh."

It seemed like an eternity passed before Stewart came back on the line. "Just spoke to Salome. She guaranteed no earlier than Monday."

"Thank you."

"Hank, don't despair too much yet. It's possible he's only going to-"

"No, it's not. But thanks for trying to make me feel better. I better get back to work. Or home, rather, since I have no work at the moment."

"Sure. I thought you did an outstanding job on the press conference, and it was a good idea to step aside for a little while. We'll keep you updated from my end."

Hank hung up the phone and turned back to his closet. He was strangely calm and focused.

"Can I talk now, Hank?" asked Rupert softly.

"Be my guest."

"We're going to find a way to get you out of this. I promise."

Hank laughed a little. "You shouldn't make promises you can't keep. I'm going home, gents. Dav, I'll call you in a little while. I have some ideas to pursue for the investigation."

Daven still said nothing. He hadn't said a word since the press conference, not even the slightest glint of approval, and it hurt Hank's feelings.

"Goodnight, guys. You okay, Dav?"

"No."

"Me either. Keep in touch, okay?"

CHAPTER TWO

Bancroft House

Tuesday morning, March 14

It was rare for Hank Bancroft to feel sorry for himself, but here he was doing exactly that. The questionnaire Stewart had sent him was intense, but by lunchtime he got halfway through it before getting completely stuck on one odd question:

On December 19 and 20, three calls were made from your cell phone to the number (303) 975-4153. Please explain the nature of these calls, including the recipient's name.

He had looked at his phone records just to be sure, and found that he had indeed made those calls. Most likely while he was at home, judging by the time they were made. But for the life of him, he couldn't remember why on earth he would have called any Denver numbers back then. He searched his email for a reference to it and found nothing. Rather than skipping this question and moving on to the next, he just sat there and stared at it for a good hour or so before picking up the phone and calling Daven.

"Hey Dav, do me a favor? Have Taylor search for some info on this number. I'll explain why later, but it should be a priority." He gave the number.

"Will do. Are you okay, Hank? Haven't heard from you all day. Sent you a couple emails."

"I know, sorry. I'll get to them right now. How are you doing?"

Daven sighed. "Remember how I said I never wanted your job? I still don't."

"I know. With any luck I'll steal it right back from you soon. I need you to stop by tonight and sign some paperwork related to your guardianship of the boys."

"Hank-"

"Don't start with me, Dav. It's just precautionary, something I should have done it a long time ago."

Long silence. "Fine. What time?"

"Whenever. Thank you."

FBI HQ - Philadelphia

"Harmon is here, sir," sang out the receptionist on Stewart's intercom.

"Send him in." Stewart slammed shut the binder on Hank Bancroft, and braced himself for an incredibly rough meeting. He couldn't stand Harmon in any shape or form, not even to watch him on TV, and he especially hated the fact that his dislike for the man caused a bias towards Hank that he couldn't control despite being completely aware of it. He knew he would have to set that aside and be completely objective, but it wasn't going to be easy.

"Welcome to Philadelphia," he said, handing Harmon a bottle of water as he walked in. "Long time no see. Please have a seat."

"Thank you." Harmon declined the bottle of water. "Brought my own, thanks."

"Alright. Let's get down to business, then. What brings you here?"

Harmon looked nervous, which was unusual. "I'm convinced that one of Hank's informants stole personal information from our databases and provided it to Hank for distribution."

"Okay. What's convincing you?"

"Our IT experts traced the listserv posting to a 10-block radius in Santa Monica. Within that radius is the Seditionists headquarters." He pulled out a notebook full of papers and handed one over to Stewart. "I'd like to ask that the FBI verify this information."

Stewart studied the map, then looked up. "You said your IT experts already traced it."

"Well, I'm hoping you have the technology to narrow it down further. Those ten blocks happen to contain hundreds of offices and homes."

"Right." Stewart took the cap off the bottle of water he had offered, and drank some himself. "You already know we have that technology."

Harmon nodded, but he didn't seem smug or victorious about any of this. Reluctant, almost. Stewart was intrigued by this remarkable change in his behavior since their last meeting, but he forced himself to stay business-like.

"May I ask why you're in such a hurry to turn it over to us? You haven't even finished your own investigation yet."

"The Urbanes are not framing Hank. I know he's accusing us, but under oath I will tell you that's not the case. I have nothing to do with this. The public, however, might not feel the same."

"Ah. I see. You're worried that public opinion is going to turn against you, and you're trying to prove your innocence before they have the chance."

"Yes."

"Which, in turn, means proving Hank's guilt before he has the chance to pin it on you."

"Yes." Harmon thought of the tape in his briefcase but left it alone for now; he needed more leverage first.

"Okay. So...you came here to ask for my help in what, exactly? Besides trying to find the exact location of the listserv posting."

Harmon shifted in his chair. "I have no doubt his agents have done harm within my organization, and that he's entirely responsible for this data leak. That's what I want to focus on. But I want to make it a civil matter, not criminal."

"You can't once the FBI is involved. You know that."

"I'm asking you to make an exception."

"Why? If you're so convinced he's guilty, then-"

"Because I don't want his kids to become Bonded Retainers, that's why," Harmon interrupted irritably. "That law is bullshit and should have never passed. We both fought it, and somehow we lost. I'm not going to let him just...just tell me, can you make an exception, or not?"

Oh, this is different . A tender side of Harmon that Stewart never knew existed.

"We might not have to make an exception. The boys have another legal guardian. If Hank is convicted by March 31, Daven likely gets custody of them. The old law allows for that if the guardian has been in place for over five years, which he has. After April 1, the courts have to approve him, and I doubt they will. Especially if he's tied up in this whole mess, or implicated in any way. I can't predict what will happen."

"So we need to do this today."

"Yes. I can order his arrest as early as tomorrow if you have definite proof of any felony that he committed. That should leave enough time to get it wrapped up by March 31."

Harmon was floored. "You're trying to rush a trial for him? One that might not leave enough time to look at all the possibilities."

Stewart nodded. "Therein lies the problem. I've been busting my ass trying to find something to help, but right now it's all just a waiting game."

Harmon stood up and started to leave. "We'll go to civil court, even if I can't prove a damned thing. Forget it. Thanks for your time."

"Harmon."

"What?" he snapped.

"Just because you're taking it to civil court doesn't mean we're going to drop our criminal investigation of all the other charges. If you prove your case there, it's going to be proved here. Possibly too late."

That gave Harmon pause. "So...what are you telling me to do?"

"I want you to tell me the truth. Do you have hard evidence that Hank committed a felony?"

Destroy the tape. This is not worth it. Hank was just joking.

Stewart saw the flash in Harmon's dark eyes, the affirmation couched in denial. "No."

"I don't believe you," he replied calmly. Quietly.

Harmon scoffed. "Well I guess we're at an impasse, aren't we?"

Stewart let a warning tone slip into his next words. "I'm sorry, I was under the impression you were trying to help Hank. My mistake."

"I am! And rushing into a trial is not the way to do it."

"I'll keep that in mind. And you should keep in mind that, as the aggrieved party, you would have the right to benefit from a plea bargain that might include being able to obtain the deed to his children."

"Oh, right. Hank Bancroft is going to waive his right to a trial, say he's guilty, and turn his children over to me while he traipses off to prison. What kind of drugs are you on? What the hell would I even do with his kids, for god's sake?"

Then...the bombshell. Stewart looked him straight in the eyes and didn't waiver. "Deeds are transferable to any free adult, Harmon. It wouldn't require the approval of a court."

That startled the man, and the sudden realization of what Stewart was secretly telling him to do seemed to hit him like a ton of bricks.

"You want me to...you...holy shit. He's going to get convicted anyway, isn't he? You already have him, but you can't move fast enough."

Stewart fought to hide the relief he felt that Harmon was figuring it out on his own, and he completely ignored the question since he had no authorization to confirm such a thing.

"You really should educate yourself better in these matters if you're thinking of pressing ahead. I would recommend pages 561 through 567 of the Courts & Law review. Might help you see things more clearly and aid in your decision. I'll have some copies made for you." He reached over to his intercom button and instructed his secretary to pull out the book and copy the pages for his "guest."

Harmon left with no further comments, and Stewart suddenly felt like crying. He desperately needed anything he could get to convict Hank as quickly as possible, and he had done the best he could to force Harmon into seeing it, too. But he was afraid that Harmon wasn't imaginative enough to read between the lines and see the full potential of their options. That he could transfer the deeds to Daven. Had he understood?

Salome came out from behind the door of the listening room. "Jesus. That was an unexpected turn of events. I got what you were implying right away, but did he?"

"I'm not sure. I could see the gears turning, but the light bulb dimmed there at the end. At any rate, I failed. He didn't leave his proof. I'm guessing I'm out of a job now, too."

"Don't be ridiculous."

The intercom lit back up again, and Stewart punched it irritably. "Yes?"

"Sir, Harmon is asking to come back in for a moment. Said he left his phone on your desk?"

There was nothing there. "Yes, he did. Tell him to come in and get it."

Harmon walked back in a minute later, and his eyes got wider upon spotting Salome. "Sorry, didn't mean to interrupt."

"That's okay. What's up?"

"I assume you were listening," he said to Salome, who nodded.

Harmon put his briefcase on the desk and unlatched the sides. "I just have one more question for you both."

"Yes?"

"Would I be able to negotiate the boys out of indentured servitude altogether?"

Salome answered. "No. The current law is that if Hank gets convicted in a state court, the minimum indenture for them is 20 years."

"Until March 31, you mean."

"Correct. After that…it's for life."

"With castration at 16, and all that fun, wholesome stuff."

Salome crossed her arms. "We didn't write the laws, Harmon, and I can certainly assure you Stewart and I don't agree with them. But yes, that is true."

"Can you guarantee we can get this done by March 31?"

"If Hank agrees to the plea bargain, yes."

Harmon opened his briefcase and handed Stewart the tape.

"Then I would like to press criminal charges against Hank Bancroft in the state of Colorado."

CHAPTER THREE

FBI HQ - Philadelphia

Same day

"I don't know, Salome, this whole thing still rings false to me. I can't accept it."

Stewart was miserably reviewing the latest transcript of the call from their mystery informant, the same one who claimed Hank Bancroft paid him to murder Janet. He hated being back to this same dreary subject. The tape Harmon had given him today wasn't the solid proof he had hoped for; no, that was a differently felony altogether and made exactly zero difference to this particular investigation. The meeting with him had led to nothing more than the same number of unanswered questions they had started with, to everyone's deep frustration.

Salome cleared her throat and rearranged her desk needlessly for the fifth time this afternoon. "Me either, but you know we have to stay objective. If we don't track down this caller, we're never getting anywhere. No clues yet at all?"

"No. I don't understand it. Why is he playing us? What does he have to gain by staying anonymous? I mean, hell, he could easily hide behind the Whistleblower Act and gain our protection rather than incriminating the hell out of himself.

This is like putting together a puzzle that's missing all the edges. I mean...look at this part."

Bancroft called me several times in the days before Christmas on a temporary phone I purchased just for this job.

Stewart sat up a little straighter, his heart pounding again. He didn't want to believe it, but he could hardly dismiss the connection without comment. "Those might be the three calls on the phone records we audited. You know, the ones we asked him about?"

"Yes. The number with a Denver area code that was deactivated the day *after* Christmas?" She reached into her desk drawer and pulled out the binder. "If this caller can verify the number, we can verify him and this whole shady story."

"He'll never give it to us. He'll think we can track down where he bought it, and therefore identify him. Not a chance."

"But we can't. We've tried already, you know that."

"But *he* doesn't know that. Salome, I think we should let him know we have the number, and tell him we can find him."

Salome stared at Stewart uncomprehendingly. "Why? Wouldn't that scare him off?"

"We should also tell him we now have surveillance video of the person who purchased the cashier's checks."

"Why?" Salome repeated.

"To force him into shitting or getting off the pot. Excuse the expression. All he's done is just throw tidbits at us and disappear. Maybe we can scare him into giving us everything all at once, so we can get this thing damned thing settled before the 31st."

Salome shook her head. "I'm sorry, but no. We're not going to resort to scare tactics. That's an old United States tactic, and we're not that anymore. We're better than them."

Stewart scoffed. " *Better*. Right. This waiting game is bullshit, Salome. You know it is. We have to move *now* . Christ, with the surveillance video coming back on Thursday we almost have everything we need except for this asshole's identity! All we need to do is confirm he really does work for the Seditionists, and this conviction is certain. That's it. And we have less than two weeks to do it before..."

He didn't have to say anything else; they both knew what was at stake.

"We wouldn't be in this position if that March 1 vote hadn't passed. But that doesn't mean we're going to resort to lower ourselves to scare tactics. Let's try something else," Salome suggested, ignoring Stewart's insolence. "Hank's convinced that Colbert is behind this, right? And he doesn't think this person actually works for him, but is just a go-between?"

Stewart nodded. "He has zero evidence, though. And so do we."

Salome smiled a little. "I'm willing to look further into the possibility anyway. Let's stop by Denver on the way to Los Angeles. If Colbert shits a brick upon hearing that we have *two* videos of our suspect as well as tracking down his phone number, we'll know he's involved."

Stewart grinned, approving of the plan, but..."That's pushing it awfully close to Monday. We're going to run out of time."

"Alright. Then we'll go tonight and meet Harmon in the morning, and Hank in the afternoon. Get packed."

Bancroft House

Tuesday night 6pm

If any moments in Hank's life had ever seemed impossible to overcome, they were now deemed inexpressibly easy compared to answering the phone when Stewart finally called with the news about what Harmon wanted. He felt as if his arms were suddenly made of lead, and the ringing was as loud as cannon fire in the confines of his study. After several long moments of pondering whether he and the boys could get away with sailing off into the wild blue yonder and disappearing, he ruefully dismissed the idea and turned bodily around in his chair to yank the phone out of its holder.

"Hello Stewart."

"Hello Hank. Got a minute?"

"Just one minute? Seems like I have the rest of my life in your hands."

Stewart hesitated, then declined to acknowledge the bitter sarcasm. "I'm really sorry to tell you that both Harmon and the FBI are moving forward with criminal charges. I'll have to arrest you on Monday. I'm sorry."

Hank counted to ten before he responded. He had never expected to be having a conversation like this, not in a million years, but here he was. Here *they* were.

"I see. Why didn't he just pursue a civil lawsuit?"

Because I made him do this, and I hate myself for it. "We'll talk more later. I'm quite limited in what I can say right now."

"Alright. Guess I'm flying to Philadelphia on Sunday night, then."

"No, anytime Monday is fine. Just arrive before midnight. Listen, I've been speaking to Salome about this whole thing for a couple hours after Harmon left, and she's insisted on interviewing Daven and Rupert first. We're actually on the way to Denver in about two hours, and tomorrow afternoon I'll need to meet with you all in Los Angeles. Separately, of course."

Alarm prickled along the hairs of Hank's neck. "What are you going to ask them?"

"Anything within our due diligence, Hank. We have to. You know that."

"They didn't do anything wrong."

"Never said they did."

Hank gulped down the last of his whiskey, but didn't even realize he was doing it. "What time?"

"I don't know yet. Maybe 2pm."

"What are the charges, exactly?"

Stewart took a deep breath. "They'll be detailed in the official subpoena I'm bringing tomorrow."

"Super. Can't wait."

Stewart paused, hating everything about every word on this conversation. He would give anything to be calling just to bitch Hank out about something stupid, like he had so many times before. A dumb, childish infraction that wouldn't lead to such a drastic end.

"There's one last thing for now. As of this moment you're officially prohibited from contacting any member of Harmon's team for any reason, by any method. If you even try it, you'll get nailed for contempt. So just don't."

"Hmmm. Would that be a felony in this context?"

"No, but it won't help your case in any way whatsoever."

Hank shrugged, the gesture unseen by his conversation partner. "Fair enough. I have no idea what I'd say, anyway. Can Daven or Rupert talk to them?"

"Not at the moment. After Monday, yes."

Another pour and drag of whiskey, and suddenly his mood turned from somber to downright foul. "Peachy. This night just keeps getting better. Are we done?"

"Yes. There's no need to be rude to-"

Hank hung up the phone and immediately hit his intercom button to staff quarters. He had one more weekend with the boys was suddenly determined to make the most of it.

"Maurice, report to my study on the double. Bring a notepad."

"Yes, sir?"

"Arrange for the boat to be transferred to Dana Point on Thursday or Friday, and then have it ready by 10am Saturday for a day sail. I'll send you a shopping list to you soon for food and drinks. You can come with us or not, your choice, but either way I need you down there getting everything set up before we go. Sorry to butt in on your weekend."

"That's alright, sir."

"Secondly, reserve 3 hotel rooms Saturday night at the Ritz-Carlton in Laguna Niguel, tickets for Disneyland on Sunday, as well as lunch and dinner reservations at Club 33. We'll also need the usual cast member escorts."

"Yes, sir."

"Cancel the banquet for Sunday. Let the hotel know we'll pay them anyway since it's late notice."

"Yes, sir. You're skipping-" Maurice stopped himself; it wasn't his place to ask, even though every fiber of his being wanted to protest. The media would tear Hank apart as a heathen come Monday if he didn't go to church. The only time they didn't was when he was down with the flu recently, in which not a single whiny protest was lodged in the papers thanks to Rupert's strongly worded request to the press.

"No, we're not skipping church," Hank replied to the unasked question, apparently unperturbed for once by Maurice's nosiness. "We'll go to Crystal Cathedral since Theo's always wanted to see it, and head to Disneyland afterwards. Lastly, the servants don't have to return home until Monday at three, including you, so reschedule the bus."

"Yes, sir."

"Thanks Maurice, that will be all for now."

The man left, and Hank wearily hit the intercom button again. "Avery. My study, please."

While he waited for his guard, Hank had about two minutes to wonder what in the hell he was going to tell Theo and Floyd. No matter how he did it, the boys would be inconsolable. What fresh hell for poor Floyd, who couldn't even see his own house on television without having a fit. The poor kid would probably end up hospitalized again, and there wasn't a damned thing Hank could do about it.

Knock, knock.

"Come in."

Avery carefully entered, still wary and wounded from having been thoroughly dressed down for saying in front of Theo that Hank should have been at the hospital with Floyd instead of at the office. He knew he deserved it and fully understood the reason for it, but that made it no easier to swallow. Hank had a ferocious way with words when he was angry, and some of his more choice phrases were still ricocheting painfully around Avery's consciousness.

Hank was calm and almost friendly, however. That was unusual, considering his incredible penchant for holding grudges longer than was reasonably acceptable. "I realize you have planned time off next week, so I would like to take Martinez with me to Philadelphia on Monday. We might have to stay for a while." *Maybe years, in my case .*

"I can go, boss," Avery said quickly, not wanting to cause any drama. "My days off start on Thursday. If we're back by then, it's fine."

"We might not be," Hank quietly responded after an awkward silence. "I can't really say why."

Oh, shit...he's done it now . "Then I should go with you. I'll change my plans. Don't worry, sir."

Hank looked immensely relieved, which perked up his guard somewhat. "Thank you. We'll also be going on a weekend trip. More details later. I have a lot to do tonight, so forgive me for being vague. You can go."

Avery ignored the dismissal and stepped forward, taking a deep breath. "Speaking of forgiveness...I sincerely hope you've forgiven me for what I said in front of Theo."

Hank looked away and rifled through a binder that was laying out on the credenza. "I'd be lying to you if I said I did," he responded, not unkindly. "But I am trying."

Avery took another deep breath, steeling himself for what he was about to say next. "Hank, when you summoned me to your office I was busy shuffling through the live camera feeds."

That got Hank's full attention again; he turned around in his chair. "And?"

"You know that I don't like to get the boys in trouble, right?"

"Yes, I know. Worst part of your job, you've said a thousand times. What's happened?"

It was true. Avery hated this part of his job. Hated it more than anything else in the world, but he had no choice. This is what he was paid for and had agreed to do. "Floyd snuck out of his room and he's in the pool house."

Hank didn't have to ask what his son was doing. He knew without question.

The intercom lit up, interrupting the conversation. Hank punched the button irritably.

"Mr. Johansson is here, sir," said Martinez, who was stationed in the guardhouse.

"I assume you let him in?"

"No, sir. Waiting for your permission."

Avery nodded approvingly; Martinez was learning fast after several early faux pas that had drawn his new boss's ire.

"Good," Hank said, approving of the caution as well. "Send him up. Thank you."

Hank turned back to Avery. "Thank you. We'll talk some more tomorrow."

"Shall I tell Floyd to-"

"No," said Hank decisively as he stood up to go deal with this latest mess. "I've got it, and I won't mention who was watching the cameras. Thanks."

"I'm sorry, Dav," Hank said grumpily as he returned to his study to his waiting friend and slammed the door behind him. "Had a slight issue with my oldest."

"Is he alright?" Dav asked with true concern, and not just out of courtesy.

Hank stopped himself from rolling his eyes in frustration. "Floyd is not allowed to watch the news without me. One guess as to what he was just doing?"

"I have no idea," Dav replied seriously, and Hank gaped at him.

"Watching the news. Really, Dav?"

"Oh. What did you do?"

Hank sat down hard. "What I had to do. The kid disobeyed a direct order; he knew what to expect. Have you made up your mind about the guardianship issue?" he barked without intending to. Daven looked aghast at him, and Hank flushed.

"Sorry. Way to launch right into business, right? Forgive me. It's been a hell of a day. Let me rephrase. Have you made a decision regarding my request to take guardianship of the boys if something happens to me?"

Dav nodded. "Of course my answer is yes. It was never going to be anything else."

"Really? Could have fooled me," Hank muttered bitterly.

Daven sat down in Hank's guest chair. "Is something wrong, Hank? Besides Floyd, of course. You seem unusually-"

"Is anything right?" Hank interrupted. "I'm going to Philadelphia on Monday. In the afternoon, specifically."

"Why? Were you summoned?"

Hank tensed, not wanting to tell Dav the truth yet, but not wanting to lie to him, either.

"Not yet. Dav...we need to have a serious talk. I don't know if right now is the time to do it, but I don't see how waiting is going to make this easier. Just be honest with me. What was the real reason you held back those receipts for so long?"

Daven took the bottle of water Hank offered. "You told me to never tell you."

"I'm asking you now. It's important."

"I'm not going to answer," Daven replied calmly as he took a drink. "Per your orders, if you don't recall. You were adamant."

"And why do you think that was, exactly?"

"Because then you would have to tell the FBI, and I'd get in trouble."

Hank felt like his world was spinning suddenly. "Fine. Then just answer yes or no: did you hold back because you didn't want it to cause bad PR and influence the vote?"

Daven stared at him coolly, expression unreadable. The guess wasn't exactly correct; he had only done it to keep Hank focused, not to distract the voters. But either way, the desired end result was essentially the same. Dav had seriously messed up, but he sincerely had not realized it until this moment. How much he had put Hank's career in jeopardy with his good intentions.

"No comment."

"Okay, let me put it this way. If that's what you did, for god's sake, *don't* tell anyone that. Attempting to influence the vote with something like that could be considered a felony. Do you understand me?"

"Loud and clear."

Hank paused breathlessly, seeing a rare burst of fear that crossed Daven's eyes for a fraction of a second like a shooting star. "*Fuck*. You did. I knew it. You've been around Rupert too long. Jesus, Dav."

Daven took another long draw of water. "Is Stewart going to interview me?"

"Yes he is. Tomorrow."

"Hank, you of all people should know I'm not going to let you take the fall for something I did."

Hank stood up and walked to his window, frustrated beyond description. "No. I am literally ordering you to keep your trap shut about the vote, understand me?"

Daven cocked his head like a quizzical beagle. "You can't order me around, Hank. I'm the one in charge now."

Hank froze, his heart in his throat. Coming from anyone else, that remark would have been an egotistical, hurtful, even threatening statement. Coming from Daven, however, it was simply the truth watered down to its barest element. He regularly made stark observations like this without any ulterior motives or malice, a fact which usually comforted Hank. This time, it didn't. He felt like breaking anything within reach suddenly, but managed to keep himself still.

"Right. Dav, you should leave before I lose my temper and say things I'm going to deeply regret."

"I'm not afraid of your temper. Besides, isn't there something I have to sign in regards to Floyd and Theo?"

Hank had forgotten all about it; now he seethed impotently as he returned to his desk and pushed the thick packet over.

"This is to accept the responsibility for handling my estate and take over complete guardianship of my sons. I'm leaving everything to you. All my property and finances, too."

Now it was Daven's turn to freeze in horror. "Hank. No. I can't."

"You can, and you will." He tapped the cover of the bound pages. "*This* is why you can't be guilty of a felony. Because then you'll have *nothing,* and neither will the boys. This is for them, not you. Now do you understand me?"

Daven looked down. Horrified, but calm. "What am I supposed to tell Stewart, then?"

"That you held back because you were afraid of confronting me after what happened at Christmas. I'm a tyrant, everyone knows that. Play that up and he'll be fine. It's what I already told him."

Daven could not meet Hank's eyes suddenly. "You're not a tyrant, and I'm not agreeing to that or signing this until you answer one simple question."

"What?"

"Are you going to Philadelphia on Monday to be arrested?"

Hank picked up his whiskey bottle again. "I thought you said it was a simple question."

"Are you?"

"Look, anything could happen between now and then. I'm just being practical and cautious."

Daven didn't back down. "Answer the question, Hank. Without drinking that entire bottle first, if you don't mind."

Hank hesitated, then swallowed another mouthful and nodded as he locked eyes with Dav. There was a very long silence between the two friends.

"When were you planning to tell me this?" Daven finally asked, astonished.

"Give me a break, Dav. I just learned about it less than hour ago and I'm still in disbelief."

"I'm sorry. What evidence do they have?"

"I don't know yet. Enough, apparently. I really don't want to talk about it right now," Hank added sullenly, hating himself for being so outwardly cold toward the man who was trying to save him and his sons. Although it made sense since part of him, Hank realized reluctantly, resented Daven for getting him into this mess in the first place by holding back the damned receipts.

Another long silence.

"Well, we need to talk at some point. Like tomorrow morning. Now everything you've been saying lately makes sense. Give me the pen, please."

Hank didn't comply yet. "Wait. What are you going to tell Stewart about the receipts?"

"Whatever you want, as long as it keeps you from taking the blame. Pen?"

Now Hank handed it over. "Thank you. Just know that there's no one else I would trust more to do this for me."

Daven nodded. "There's one more thing. I don't think you should send the boys to Maui."

"Why not?"

"I want them with me," Daven insisted.

"You'll be at work. That makes no sense."

"It makes a hell of a lot more sense than sending them away and disappearing, and leaving Millie to deal with the aftermath. She doesn't know them as well as I do."

Hank almost immediately launched into to a protest, but then he remembered something crucial: Daven's own father had left the family without a trace years ago. Hank backed off immediately, knowing what a sensitive and painful subject that was for his dear friend. He suddenly had no desire to inflict the same agony upon his own sons.

"You're right. She won't know how to handle Floyd. Can they stay with you next week? I'll have Maurice connect with you guys and do all the shopping, and Chef can come by and do the cooking."

"Or I can just stay in your house. It will be less disruption for the boys, and more private."

"Yeah. Good idea. If you don't mind, let's just do that for as long as necessary."

"Any idea how long that might be?" Daven prodded anxiously.

"Anywhere between one day and forever, I guess," Hank said offhandedly as he tore open a huge bag of peanut M&Ms.

Daven stared aghast at him, the serious of the situation suddenly cloaking his heart in a frozen, tangible heaviness.

"For god's sake, Hank. It seems an odd choice to be so flippant about this."

"I can either be flippant, or I can be hysterical. Let's just try to stay positive, okay?" Hank replied quietly, mouth and hands full of chocolate. "Want some?"

"No, thank you."

Daven turned back to the packet with a deep sigh and quietly signed the papers. Much to Hank's relief, he didn't notice the clause that automatically turned custody of the boys and all his property and finances over to him at 11:59pm on March 31 if Hank wasn't free by then.

A few minutes later the enormous deed was done, and both men didn't know what to say to each to other.

“Thanks, Dav,” Hank managed, heart lodged firmly in his throat. "Want to stay for dinner?”

 “I would like to, but my appetite is completely gone and I'm fairly certain you wouldn't enjoy my company right now. Thank you, though. Can we please talk in the morning?”

“I'm busy until noon or so. I’m sorry that I’ve been keeping you out of the loop. My four informants are meeting me here in the morning. It’s crucial that their identities are protected, so I have to keep you out of it.”

Daven shrugged. “You don’t think Harmon will suddenly notice four of his people have disappeared from the office in the same week you recalled your agents? They won’t stay secret for long.”

“You’re right. But I’d like to just talk to them alone, okay? I’ll fill you in later and give you names so we can relocate them to our office. Call me at noon.”

“Alright. Goodnight, Hank. I implore you not to give up yet. We’ve still got a long way to go with our investigation.”

Hank nodded. “I know. Thank you. Um, on another subject altogether, do you remember that code to dial when you want your caller ID to be blocked?”

“I think it’s star six seven. Why?”

“I just want to make a quick call to a restaurant but don’t want my number to get out again. Thanks."

Daven left, and the moment the door shut, Hank snatched up his phone and dialed Harmon, taking care to block his number first.

Denver, Colorado

Harmon usually never answered unknown callers, but cell service at the Denver airport was infamously spotty, and with his lack of technical savvy he thought perhaps some kind of signal weakness was preventing the number from coming through. He did make sure not to say his real name, however...just in case.

"Hello?"

"Hi, handsome. How's your day been?"

"Who is this?"

"Who do you think?" answered the gruff voice on the other line.

Harmon found himself breathless all of a sudden as he got into his car on the tarmac. "Ah. If you're calling to threaten me again-"

"Not at all," Hank replied easily. "On the contrary, I'm calling you with a friendly reminder."

"You're not in the position to be reminding me of anything right now, *friend*."

"Oh, I think I am. Code 314.3 of the political integrity code prohibits our parties from releasing names of our own employees, as well as those of each other's parties. Speaking of which, you're going to be missing four people at roll call tomorrow. Just wanted to give you a head's up."

Harmon felt his throat go dry. "Your informants, I gather."

"Right on. As a *friend*, I just wanted to make sure you didn't get your little hands slapped for doing something so silly and preventable like publicizing who they were to anyone outside the need-to-know group."

"Duly noted."

"Good, good," Hank answered, his tone obnoxiously chipper. "Well, you're welcome. I'm looking forward to reconnecting with them tomorrow. No doubt they'll have a lot to tell me about their time spent in your wonderful organization, so thank you for confirming you'll help keep them safe. Have a nice evening."

"Hank, wait-"

The line went dead.

CHAPTER FOUR

Tuesday night, Bancroft House

"Well, that was a really stupid thing to do, asshole," Theo said matter-of-factly after Floyd finished explaining where he'd been and why his eyes were red, even though he did feel sorry for his brother in spite of it all.

Floyd threw his hands up in frustration and flopped around on Theo's bed to face the wall. "I knew you wouldn't have any sympathy, bitch. I'm freakin' sixteen years old, but he keeps treating me like I'm twelve!"

"More like five, but act like a dumbass and you're going to get your dumb ass whooped. It's not rocket science."

"Okay, Theo. You can stop now." Floyd didn't say it, but he wasn't mad about the consequences he'd just received; he was only indignant about being kept so isolated from the outside world. Furious about what he had just learned from the mouth of someone who didn't even know him.

"Here he comes," Theo said quietly, reaching over to mute his video game as the sound of a heavy footfall on the stairs made its way into the bedroom. Floyd didn't move, he only stiffened as Hank entered the room like a shark searching for his next prey.

"Dinner's ready, boys. Sorry it's late, I had to meet with Uncle Dav. Go downstairs," Hank said tiredly, keeping his eyes on his oldest. Theo went, but Floyd didn't move, as Hank expected. He waited a long moment, then sat down next to him and rested his arm on Floyd's side, patting him reassuringly.

"Okay. You can stop pouting now, kiddo. It's over and done with."

"It's not over," Floyd muttered.

"Excuse me? Did you not hear me say you're forgiven?"

"But I haven't forgiven *you* yet. You said I could watch, then I couldn't. You're an Indian giver."

Hank's heart fell a little, and his resolve hardened even further as he took a tight grip on Floyd's forearm. "Don't use that phrase ever again. It's racist. And I thought you understood where I was coming from in regards to the news. Do I need to repeat myself?"

"Please don't," Floyd grumbled as he shifted his weight around into a somewhat more comfortable position. "Or else I'll be forced to poke out my own eardrums, I swear."

Hank held back a snigger. Floyd had a tendency to be unintentionally amusing when he was this pissed, which was doubly unfortunate because also he hated being laughed at. Especially when he was angry. It was a fine line to tread, so

Hank tried to inject some lightness into his tone without going overboard.

"Well, we don't want that, it's messy. I won't say a word. What did you learn from your little expedition today, then? Any juicy news about myself that I should know? I mean, sometimes Hailey knows what's up before I do, so maybe you can give me a briefing of what's going on in the life of Hank Bancroft."

"Don't know. I only got to watch like five minutes before Avery narced on me."

"What did you learn in those 5 minutes?"

Floyd hesitated, not knowing whether his dad was baiting him or genuinely trying to find out what the headlines were. His tone was bitter when he finally answered. "The Santa Anas are blowing."

Hank glanced out the window automatically; it was pitch dark but he could easily imagine his palm trees tipping over quite a bit from the infamous windstorms that periodically sapped the sanity out of Los Angeles residents for days at a time

"Air moves sometimes. Huh. Who would've thought?" Hank was secretly relieved; that meant he wasn't at the top of the ticker for once. *But not for long.*

"That really hurt, dad," Floyd complained in a mumble as he rubbed his backside; his efforts to dull the sting becoming more fruitless with each passing minute.

Hank was not sorry, not one bit. "It was supposed to. Kiddo, you knew exactly what was going to happen the moment you turned on that television. Did you really expect me to go easy on you when we've been through this twice before? Stop pouting and come down to dinner."

"I'm not eating again until you let me watch the news on my own."

"Since when did you start giving me ultimatums? I don't think so." He gripped Floyd's shoulder as he stood. "Attitude ends now. Up. I won't tell you again. Food's getting cold."

Philadelphia Airport - Tuesday evening

"You know, I've been thinking," began Salome as she stuffed her carry-on suitcase into the overhead bin. "You're exactly right. We need to ask our caller what that mobile phone number is. Or was, rather. I mean we already have it, right? So whether or not he gives it to us, he's in the same boat as far as possibly being tracked goes."

"I'm not following, sorry."

Stewart sat down in his window seat, glad for once that he didn't have a stranger seated next to him all the way to Denver. He wanted to talk to Salome. Needed to talk to her and find any way out for Hank.

Salome dropped down into her seat and deftly snapped the seatbelt shut. "I mean we tell him we have the number, but unless he can confirm it's the same one, we are no longer taking his calls seriously. When you think about it, that makes the tracking issue irrelevant."

"Shit or get off the pot, like I said," Stewart answered wryly.

"Precisely. When he calls back, you have to ask him. Give him part of the number outright so he knows we're not bluffing, and ask him to finish it. If he can't, we simply won't take his calls any longer. End of story, investigation over and whatever he's trying to gain now is all lost."

"Right. The problem is, I almost don't want him to be able to verify it. That would mean he's not lying."

"I know," Salome agreed glumly. "Just keep in mind that Janet deserves justice, and it's our duty to get it for her. Let's just hope he calls back sooner than March 31."

Bancroft House - same evening

"Boys," Hank said heavily, with a rapidly pounding heart as they finished off the last of their burgers. It had taken him almost half an hour to get up the courage to even address the matter at all. "I have to go to Philadelphia on Monday, and I'll likely be there all week. Uncle Dav is going to come and stay with you guys here. I fully expect a glowing report of your perfect behavior when I get back."

Floyd's eyes were wide, and he was frozen in a state of lifting a chip to his mouth. "You've never been gone that long. What's going on?"

Tell him the truth. "There are some meetings I have to go to," he said with a dry throat, absurdly self-conscious of how stilted he sounded. "There's also an investigation ongoing that I'm a part of, which requires me to answer and ask lot of questions. It will take time due to all the people involved."

"An investigation about what?"

"My, my. Aren't we demanding today? An investigation, period. That's all you need to know for now."

"I want to know everything," Floyd insisted stubbornly.

"Too bad," Hank replied simply, cocking his eyebrows with a *don't push me* expression.

Floyd put down his chip and stood up quickly; it reminded Hank of all the times Maurice had suddenly stopped in his tracks to wonder if he had unplugged something or another.

"What are you doing?" Theo asked, puzzled.

"I don't feel good." He all but ran off, and Hank followed him to his room while Theody remained seated in confusion, staring after them with a pickle hanging out of his mouth.

"Floyd? What's wrong with you?" Hank asked irritably as the boy dodged him several times on the stairs. He obviously wasn't upset about his stomach. "Stop."

Floyd ran into his room and slammed the door, and locked it behind him. In the past, that would have caused Hank to all but blow a gasket. But he had his keys in his pocket, so he calmly took them out and opened the door. Floyd was in the bathroom, sitting on the edge of the tub with his face in his hands, and Hank shut the door and sat down placidly on the toilet next to him.

"Did the food make you lose your mind on top of making you sick? Don't you ever slam the door on me again, much less lock it."

"Mmmm," Floyd replied noncommittally, shoving his chin deeper down into his jacket.

After about thirty seconds of nothing but silence and heavy breathing, Hank had a feeling he knew what the real problem was and braced himself as he asked quietly, "The news. Was it really five minutes of talking about the Santa Anas?"

Floyd didn't answer at first, but he shook his head after some hesitation. *Fuck.*

"Okay. Tell me exactly what you heard. It may not be accurate and you could be getting yourself all upset over nothing."

"Yoone gaijins cical prisad cax aded."

Hank reached up and pulled Floyd's hands away from his face. "I didn't catch that. What?"

"Nothing," the stricken teenager amended.

"Floyd," Hank admonished, fighting back his own panic and dread. "It's important to me that you get the truth directly from the source, rather than some half-assed reporters. What did you hear?

Floyd ignored the question again. "If you really go to jail, does Uncle Dav become our new dad?"

Hank's pulse started thudding painfully at his temples. "Don't jump to conclusions, and please tell me you didn't breathe a word of this to Theo."

"Of course not. But does he?"

"Just try to relax. You don't even have the facts yet. Tell me what-"

Hank watched aghast as his son turned and threw up in the tub several times. He patted him on the back reassuringly until he was done, then handed him a towel from the etagere. Floyd snatched it out of his hands.

"I told you so," Floyd said frankly as he wiped his mouth. He was calm. Too calm.

"That you didn't feel good? I'm sorry. I'll go get you something for your stomach."

"No. I meant...that you should have quit your job a long time ago. You wouldn't listen." Floyd shook his head again. "You never listen."

Ouch. Hank stared at his oldest in consternation. "Floyd, this is really not helpful. Are you alright? In any pain? Do you need to go to the doctor?"

The boy tipped his head against the wall, his eyes glassy and moist, staring at nothing. "No. I told you so," he repeated softly. "I *knew* it was too late."

Hank rubbed his temples vigorously. This was all going to hell in a hand basket, and there was nothing he could do about it. No way to placate his son or make this any better. All he could do was acknowledge his increasing irritation at Floyd for disobeying his orders not to watch the news. At least the boy's color was coming back into his cheeks.

"Alright, you seem fine. You're sixteen now, as you keep reminding me, so if you want to discuss this as adults then we should do it. I'll tell you as much as I can. Let me know when you're ready,"

Floyd stood up a little shakily, but self-assured and confident, having collected himself admirably in record time. "I'm fine, sir. I don't need to talk, but thank you for the offer."

"Right. Well, it's only seven-thirty. Maybe you'll change your mind. Do you have homework?"

"I already did it, sir."

Hank fought the urge to roll his eyes. "Stop with the *sir* thing, Floyd. I hate when you resort to theatrics. I don't want to fight with you, especially over something as important as this. Go do something constructive, or educational, or-"

"Something educational? Like watching the news?" Floyd retorted mockingly.

Hank eyed him dangerously. "You're one more smart remark away from me taking off my belt again, kiddo," he warned quietly.

That was all it took to set Floyd straight; he swallowed hard and forced himself back in check again. Hank saw the fight drain out of him instantly, his eyes soft again. *There, that's better.*

"Thank you. If you really feeling alright, go drink a glass of water. Then it's bedtime and lights out. You need rest. We'll talk some more tomorrow."

"I'm fine." Floyd sighed as he went...but at least he went at all, Hank told himself.

This day was a fucking nightmare.

Bancroft House - Wednesday - 8:30am

Floyd was still nauseated and pale the next morning, so Hank let him stay home from school with the caveat that he was restricted to his room until 11:30am. That was because the informants arrived precisely as scheduled at 8:30, and Hank sat them all down nervously in the library and locked the door. Before saying a word, he walked around handed them all water bottles. They looked exactly as anxious as he felt.

"Welcome back to Los Angeles, team," he said carefully as he sat down and pulled the cap off his favorite pen and flipped open his notebook. "You've obviously already realized your presence will be missed in Denver, but Harmon's been warned not to name names. At any rate, since you went under pseudonyms, nothing should happen even if he does. Thank you again for your services. No matter what happens in the next three hours, you are all guaranteed a full relocation package, a job in the organization, and compensation for your little side job. So let's get to it and not waste any time. Mick, I'll start with you since we've spoken most recently. What's been happening in the legal department these days?"

The man cleared his throat twice before he could speak. "It's been quiet, Mr. Bancroft. Ever since Harmon got his last warning and censure, he's been stopping most litigation and offering settlements to almost everyone just to clear the slate. I don't believe anything's going to be pending that's going to be of help to you right now. But I did happen to be one of three people who had access to the papers filed against you, and learned something interesting right off the bat."

Hank sat up straight, forgetting all about writing anything down. "What's that?"

"He's got a…maybe we should speak in private?"

"No. I trust you all implicitly. Go ahead."

"Yes, sir." Mick opened his briefcase and pulled out what looked like maybe a couple dozen pages stapled together and looked around the room. "I…let's just say I trust you all implicitly, as well. We've been through a lot in the past seven or eight years. Anyway, I had a feeling we'd be recalled, so I took a copy of the attorney-client privileged draft complaint. It will help you mount your defense far ahead of the trial."

Hank didn't move, not that he could even if he wanted to. He cocked his head towards the back of the room. "There's a shredder in the corner. Feed it in there, and leave this room. You should have never-"

"Sir, I haven't read it myself, I just took-"

Hank's voice was like ice and fire all at once. "Stop talking. You should've *never* brought that here. I ought to turn you in myself. Come with me, please. Leave that face down on the chair for a moment. Nobody touch it."

Mick did, and stood up somewhat unsteadily as Hank led him directly across the hall and into his study.

"I'm so sorry, Mr. Bancroft. I meant well. Please don't-"

"Did you make a second copy?" Hank interrupted quietly after he'd shut the door behind him.

Mick looked like he didn't want to answer, but Hank asked again, and he nodded grimly. "Yes. It's in a secret pocket in my briefcase."

"Good. Shred the one on the chair in front of the others. I don't care how much we trust them, we're keeping this to ourselves. As you leave the house, place the other copy in the drawer of the side table by the front door. And even though I'm going to give you a big fat bonus for it, don't ever do this again. Got it?"

Mick nodded, so they went back into the room, and he dutifully picked the papers back up and fed them into the shredder.

"Thank you, Mick," said Hank coldly, resuming his authoritative demeanor and throwing eye daggers at the man. "We'll pretend this never happened. Please confirm there are no other existing copies."

"No, sir," the man replied shakily. "You can look through my briefcase, if you'd like. In fact, please do so that there's no suspicion later. It would make me feel a lot better."

"I won't, since it's my ass on the line. Pamela, would you do the honors?"

Pamela obviously didn't want to, but she complied and searched it thoroughly in full view of the others. Much to Hank and Mick's relief, she did not find the hidden pocket.

"It's clear, sir," Pamela finally declared.

"Good. Then this incident is forgotten and forgiven. You may leave now, Mick."

The man silently packed up his things while the others watched breathlessly. On the way out he muttered, "I'm sorry," once more. Just loud enough for everyone to hear. Hank nodded approvingly, then looked around the room and took a deep breath.

"Alright. Don't repeat his mistake, ladies. No more felonies in this room. If you have any, keep them to yourself. Who'd like to go next?"

Seditionists Headquarters, Los Angeles - 9am

"Tell me you found something, Taylor. Anything."

Taylor handed the report to Rupert. "The number comes back as disconnected on December 26. It's not traceable, unfortunately. I've been working on it for 16 hours straight and...nothing."

Daven took the report away from Rupe. "There's *nothing* we can do? At all?"

Taylor shook her head. "Maybe one day the technology will give us the ability, but right now it's a dead end. The only option would be to check the surveillance footage of every single cell phone store in the 303 area code. There are 435 of them, and we don't even have the time frame in which the phone was first activated. Needle in a haystack, gents."

Rupe shrugged. "Well, maybe the FBI can figure it out. Let's get back to work, then. Thanks, Taylor."

Urbane Headquarters, Denver - 9:30am

Salome carefully studied Colbert's face and body language while Stewart falsely claimed to have two surveillance videos on the subject, as well as a confirmed phone number and voice recording.

The big man didn't show any signs of distress at the news. Not a single tell, nothing to indicate he was in the least bit alarmed at the suspect being unveiled. If anything, Colbert looked completely bored by the proceedings altogether.

He's not involved, Salome silently concluded with sudden clarity and reluctance. Harmon wasn't responsible, either, that much was already certain. She knew with just one glance that Stewart was thinking exactly the same thing based on Colbert's lack of reaction:

Fuck...what now?

Bancroft House, 10am

"Hey buddy," Avery said as he rose from his desk when Floyd came down the stairs. "You feeling any better yet?"

Floyd was putting on his jacket and backpack. "I'm fine. Take me to Rupert's house."

Avery looked at him askance. "No. You're supposed to be in your room until 11:30. Back upstairs, and get a move on."

"Or what? You'll narc on me again?" Floyd challenged rudely. "You used to like me."

Avery tipped his head to the side slightly, willingly allowing the deep hurt and frustration he felt to show on his face and in his voice. He was simply done with this kid lately.

"You're right, I used to like you. Back when you listened to me and let me help you out. I don't feel bad about narcing on spoiled brats who disrespect me, though. Are you going back upstairs, or not?"

The deeply ashamed look on Floyd's face at this unprecedented outburst satisfied him immensely.

"I'm sorry," Floyd said hoarsely. "I don't....I didn't mean it."

"Then go upstairs," Avery responded sternly, worried that Hank would suddenly exit his library and come upon this little scene.

"Okay. Sorry." Floyd turned and ran back up the stairs. It wasn't until he let out his breath that Avery realized he'd been holding it. Two hours later when he returned to his desk in the hallway, he was pleasantly surprised to find a brief thank you note from Floyd on his keyboard. He read it, then glanced aside into the dining room, where the teenager was just sitting down to lunch with his dad. Floyd was watching him, so Avery smiled a little and gave a thumbs up.

Floyd nodded and turned his attention back to his father. He was a good kid, Avery knew. Always had been

CHAPTER FIVE

Wednesday afternoon

Urbane Headquarters - Denver - 1pm CST

Harmon was eager to get this meeting over with, and not just because he hated the FBI. Stewart, in particular, who always seemed over-eager to push his buttons. But this time it was Salome who was testing his patience with her long checklist of open-ended questions. They seemed to be almost near the end of list, much as Harmon was near the end of his patience. He was also starving.

Salome didn't seem aware of her interviewee's desires whatsoever, and she persisted without pausing. "Next. You're aware you have Seditionist informants in this specific office, I understand."

"Had. Yes."

"And if they become known, it's against the law for you to release their names outside of a need-to-know...wait a minute. What do you mean, *had?* Past tense?"

Harmon frowned. "Hank assured me there were only four, and they would be gone today and not replaced. We have exactly four employees missing today. He keeps his word, if nothing else."

Salome could feel Stewart's eyes on her. "I see. When did you have this discussion, exactly? It's strange you never mentioned it before."

"Because I was waiting for you to ask. We talked last night, very briefly."

"You called him?"

"No. He called my cell. Around seven-thirty, I think. Something like that."

"You're just as forbidden as he is to communicate. Why did you pick up the phone?"

"Didn't know it was him. He blocked his number."

Salome tapped her pen on her teeth.

"Show me."

Harmon pulled out his mobile phone, scrolled down to the "calls received" list, and handed it to her wordlessly. She looked at it, wrote something down, then handed the phone back.

"Thank you. So, you've figured out who the four employees are, correct?"

The man scowled and nodded. "Their identities will remain confidential, I assure you."

"Excellent. Will you please excuse me for a moment? I need to confer with my colleague to see if there's anything else we need to ask. Then we'll be out of your hair."

"Certainly. Please use my conference room." He stood up and opened a door for them, which led to a small conference room with no other doors. Very private, but they still walked over to the far side of the wall in an abundance of caution.

Salome whispered, "I thought you told Hank not to contact him?"

Stewart flailed his hands in frustration. "I did, about an hour prior to him doing it. I even sent him an email shortly afterwards saying the same. He knew better."

"Christ," Salome muttered. "And Harmon's just sitting there, smug as a Cheshire cat with that same knowledge. I'm going to strangle Hank."

"Not if I get to him first. At least there's no *actual* proof he called."

"Right. So do you believe Colbert is involved with this whole payments business?"

Stewart shifted uncomfortably from one foot to the other. "Based on his body language alone? No, I saw nothing to indicate he has anything at stake here, other than obvious satisfaction at watching Hank go down. Makes my stomach turn."

"Mine too. This is such a cluster fuck."

Stewart sighed heavily. "Salome, I think we should ask about those four employees. What departments they were in, at least. If even one of them had access to all that leaked information, it could be damning. I'm hoping none of them did, but I'd rather know sooner than later."

"You're right. Anything else?"

"Not that I can think of."

They went back in the room and sat down. Salome purposely didn't touch her pen or notebook to ask the next question. "Harmon...about these four employees. Were any of them high-level enough to have access to the information that got leaked about your 20 executives?"

Harmon scoffed. "High level? Hardly. All four of them are administrative assistants. Unfortunately, one was assigned to the legal department and had access to some of the documents we filed yesterday in regards to the case."

Despite his horror, Stewart had to take a private moment to appreciate and admire the fact that Hank had managed to install not one, but *four* assistants within the company. Not executives, as he had suspected. It was a brilliant stroke. After all, Hank himself was the one who single handedly brought the country to its knees while working as a lowly, underpaid office clerk for Colbert. He knew firsthand what kind of access to information these positions really had. And how no one would ever suspect their lowest-level employees could even wield such power.

Salome seemed to be thinking the same, but she kept the conversation on track. "Right. So to repeat the question, did any of them have access to the information that got leaked?"

Colbert answered for his boss. "Collectively, yes. Each of them had access to some part of it."

"I see." Salome redirected her attention back to Harmon. "So you seem to think the four were working together. Were they close friends, by chance?"

"How would I know?"

"Right. There's very little we can do without proof of an actual crime. If you find any, let us know. Do you have any further question before we take our leave?"

Harmon looked at Colbert. "Will you give us a moment, please?"

Colbert scowled, but complied. Stewart and Salome held their breaths as Harmon leaned back in his chair and studied them aggressively for a few moments.

"I want to be clear on something, just in case it's been lost in translation. I don't give a fuck about Hank Bancroft after all the grief he's given me in ten years. I've almost lost my job because of him how many times? But that doesn't mean I'm taking any pleasure in watching this all go down. Even if he's guilty as hell, this is not something that satisfies me on any level."

Stewart nodded. "We know. No one's accusing you of enjoying this."

"What I *do* care about are his sons. I have children of my own, as you know. Are we going to be able to wrap this up by March 31, or not? Because you said we could, but this...this is taking us nowhere fast. I'm getting concerned that you might have misled me."

Salome took a deep breath. "You were not misled, but that brings me to the next question. You have some work to do in regards to constructing your plea bargain. Why haven't you started it yet?"

Harmon scoffed. "There's one small detail that you might have overlooked. How am I supposed to get Hank to agree to it if you won't let me talk to him and explain my reasoning?"

"You won't. You *cannot* contact each other again, period. That's the law."

"What am I supposed to do, then? By the time I can talk to Daven and Rupert, *they* won't be able to speak to Hank, either. He'll never agree to it, and I can't exactly write in there what I'm planning to do with the deeds or else everyone will see right through this whole charade."

Salome shrugged. "Then I suggest you choose your 3rd-party negotiator wisely. Someone Hank trusts would be a good start. That's how you can get through to him after Monday."

Harmon all but threw up his hands. "Are you nuts? Hank would never trust anyone I'd be willing to name as my negotiator."

"Figure it out. I can't get involved in your strategy. We're supposed to remain neutral, and that's what I intend to do."

"You…" Harmon looked irate, but his voice was even. "You all but *forced* me to do this. I didn't want to take it this far. And now you're just going to just leave and tell me to *figure it out*?"

Salome looked unmoved. "You made your bed, and now you have to lie in it. Nobody asked you to come to Philadelphia in the first place. Any further questions?"

"No." Harmon stood up, conversation over. "With all due respect, feel free to get the fuck out of my office now."

"That went well," Stewart muttered as they got in their car to go to the airport. "Can I ask you something? With all due respect, of course," he added facetiously, in mock salute to Harmon.

"Of course."

"Why did you...why did you taunt him at the end? Maybe taunt isn't the right word. I was just surprised that the conversation took such an ugly turn."

"Unpleasantly surprised, I gather," Salome remarked with a smirk. "You seemed to be upset with me."

"Yes, actually. I feel like that did more harm than good. Do you mind letting me in on your reasoning, so that we're on the same page?"

"Sure. It's simple. I'd much rather have him pissed off at us than have him pissed off at Hank. Whose side do you think he's on now?"

"Oh." Stewart smiled widely. " *Oh* . Nice."

"Right. What's that saying you like so much?"

"Shit or get off the pot?"

"Yes. He hasn't done a damn thing since we last talked on Monday. Bet you anything he's already making a list of possible negotiators to help Hank, even as he's cursing at our backs. I may have given him a stroke, but it was exactly what he needed to hear."

"I'm impressed."

"Thank you. Call Hank, if you don't mind. Let him know we'll be at the office by 2:30. I want to meet with Rupert first, then Daven. That will leave Hank for last and give us all the time we need."

Stewart pulled out his phone. "I'll bet you a million bucks he coached Daven on what to say to us about those receipts. Or rather, what not to say."

"I don't bet on bargains, sorry."

Urbane HQ - Denver - one hour later.

"Lester Boyd. Harmon here. Long time no talk. How have you been?"

Startled silence. "Holy...I mean, hello, sir. Fine, thanks. You?"

"Good, good. Listen, I need you to come to Denver to meet with me. I can't explain over the phone. Are you available Friday? I'll send my plane for you."

"Yeah, uh...got some meetings to cancel, nothing major. Is everything alright?"

"Can you get to Richmond airport at...let's say 6:30am? It's a three-hour flight. That will put you in our offices by 8am my time, and we'll make sure to get you back in time for dinner."

"That works. Is there anything I need to prepare or read up on, or anything?"

"No. Just be at the Signature terminal as agreed. We'll talk when you get here, but not until then. Understood? And obviously, this is extremely confidential. I'll call your boss now to make an explanation for your absence."

"Great, thanks. See you Friday."

"Good. Thank you."

CHAPTER SIX

Wednesday afternoon

Bancroft House

As much as Hank wanted to eat lunch, his anxiety entirely prevented him from achieving that goal. He kept busy pushing his food all around his plate and not accomplishing much otherwise, except adding to his worries. Floyd was in the same boat but Hank had never been the type of parent to insist that his children eat everything, or not waste food they were given; in fact he was quite the opposite and had a standing agreement that Chef could indulge them with whatever they wanted. Except for Theo's sugar addiction, of course, which Hank kept under tight control. It was a wonder neither of the boys weighed 300 pounds at this point, but both of them were lean and generally made good choices.

"How are you feeling?" Hank asked suddenly, breaking the silence.

"Fine, dad, thank you."

"Not hungry?"

"Not really."

"Me either." Hank poked at his chicken again and let his thoughts wander to the lawsuit papers in the side table. He couldn't decide whether he should read the illicit document before or after he met with the FBI. If he waited, he couldn't give away anything to indicate that he had them...which is what he was afraid of if he did read them in advance. But then again, knowing in advance what he was up against could help-

"Can I go to Rupert's house after this?" Floyd queried.

"No."

That was the end of that. Floyd started to roll his eyes but stopped at his dad's warning glance, and got up to take his dishes into the kitchen instead.

"Sit down, Floyd." His tone was telling, and the teenager took a deep breath as he complied.

"Dad, I really don't want to talk right now. I'm sorry."

Hank took a huge gulp of root beer. "Wasn't asking you to talk. I have a meeting this afternoon that's going to determine what happens come Monday. Honestly, at this point, I have no idea what the hell to expect. But I promise I'll keep you in the loop, okay? I don't want you watching the news because it's going to scare the shit out of you. They love to exaggerate everything, and even lie outright, and you know that."

"So I've heard." Floyd's reply was obviously meant to be humorous based on his expression, which was not challenging, so Hank let it go without comment.

"I'm going to leave the house at two for the office, and I'm taking Avery with me. I trust you not to disobey me again."

Floyd looked down at his hands. "I won't. What time will you guys be back?"

"Around six. Come to think of it...do you want to go see a movie while I'm gone?"

"Wow, dad. You're letting me skip school to go to the movies? Are you feeling okay?"

"Just marvelous." Hank stood up and folded up his napkin, and Floyd followed suit. "I'll tell Brittany to take you to the Cineramadome." That was where the Bancrofts were allowed to use the back entrance and go in and out of movies unseen. "Then I need to go to my study and prepare for this meeting."

"Who are you meeting with?"

Raised eyebrow. "Floyd."

"You said you'd keep me in the loop," Floyd reminded him politely.

Hank sighed. "Right. I did. The FBI, and Rupe and Dav."

He worried Floyd would throw up again, but the boy merely nodded. "Okay. Good luck, dad."

"Thanks, kiddo. Go change."

Hank ventured downstairs to talk to Brittany, and stopped in his tracks when he saw she was watching the national news. Naturally, his own face was plastered onto the screen.

"Oh god," he moaned as he walked in. She jumped up and grabbed the remote to mute it, as if she were just as forbidden to watch as Floyd. But on the contrary, all the guards were expected to be on top of the latest whispers about their boss and they often had the news running all day down in the basement. Usually with the captions on so it didn't drive them crazy.

"Sorry, sir," she said, swallowing hard.

"That bad, huh? Put it back on. And I've told you a hundred times not to apologize for doing your job."

He sat partially on her desk and braced himself for what he was about to hear.

- expected to defend himself against what appears to be multiple charges laid by the Urbanes, the details of which we do not yet have. Sources from inside the party state that at least one indisputable felony charge is pending, and a statement from the FBI is still yet to be released. Calls made to Rupert Aster, PR leader for The Seditionists, were not immediately returned. We'll come back to this story as it develops.

The shot changed to the front of the house - or walls and roof, rather - where a news media truck was parked at the bottom of the driveway. Hank had seen the top of its satellite dish on his way down the stairs. He crossed his arms.

"That wasn't too awful. What else were they saying?"

Brittany looked rather wild-eyed at the question. Hank never spoke about such things with his guards. Idle discussion amongst them about Hank's work life was strictly off-limits if it didn't relate to security issues, with special consequences for those who engaged in outright gossip - as Avery had recently found out when Hank docked him an entire paycheck for his comments at the hospital.

"Well…" she hesitated, then shut her mouth tightly as Avery rounded the corner and came into the office, stopping in his tracks at the sight of Hank.

"Sorry, boss. Didn't see you."

"Stay. Welcome to the party," Hank said wryly. "It's okay, Brittany. Just tell me."

"Boswin News is saying you'll be put in jail next week, but seem to have no idea why," Brittany replied shakily. "It's been breaking news all day, with no substance. Our local news hasn't said anything. The Denver news is going a bit nuts with speculation, but again, nothing confirmed."

Avery and Brittany both couldn't meet his eyes, Hank noticed. He didn't blame them. "They mention anything about me going to Philadelphia on Monday to be arrested?"

Both of them nodded hesitantly, but made no verbal reply.

Hank replied matter-of-factly, "What a historic occasion...first damned time they've ever told the truth. Whatever happens, your jobs are safe, so don't worry. Daven is going to stay with the boys while I'm gone, however long I'm gone. They'll need you. End of story. Brittany, can you take Floyd to the movies, please? Avery, I have to go to the office at two."

"Of course," they said together, and Hank made his exit abruptly, knowing he was being an ass by casually throwing out a shocking statement like that, but at least the incident made up his mind for him. He grabbed the papers out of the side table and made his way up to his bedroom with a newly hardened resolve.

Colbert's Car - Denver

"Hey, Colbert. Sorry I took so long to call you back."

"You shouldn't be calling me at all now that you're not working. How long did Bancroft suspend you guys?"

Yannick coughed in surprise, then amusement. "Suspend? That implies some kind of wrongdoing. We were placed on administrative leave. Paid, may I add? So I'm doing a lot better than you right now."

"Well it's a damned good thing you didn't go pick up those cashier's checks yourself. FBI has the surveillance video."

"Ha. Told you so. They can track anything. So what do you want me to do next?"

Colbert waited until someone passed behind his car and out of sight again before responding. "Not much you can do at the moment. How long are you kicked out of the office for?"

"No idea. And they're probably going to poly us all before they bring us back. Hope I can pass it twice. It was hard enough not breaking a sweat the first time around. Hey…how did you know they have the video?"

"Just got out of a meeting with the FBI. They also have the number you paged Hank with. They're all over him like white on rice, and he did exactly what I expected him to. Going to have me a visit to see the man in jail, finally."

There was a pause on the other line. "*Finally?* How long have you been planning this?"

Colbert smiled to himself. "Twelve years? Ever since he first stabbed me in the back. I have stories, my man. Stories for days. Hard to believe it's almost over."

Yannick bit the inside of his cheek. Something about this wasn't right, suddenly. Everything was...perhaps very wrong, perhaps not. Maybe he was just being paranoid.

"I see. So this isn't exactly all a business venture, then?" he asked lightly.

"All you need to know is that I've got more than enough cash to keep you going until it's done. And I'll be in touch again when I need something else."

"Don't you mean *we?*" Yannick asked quickly. "You and Harmon?"

"Of course." Colbert started a little when he looked into his rearview mirror and saw Umber come into the garage. "Got to go."

There was no getting out of the man seeing him, so Colbert quickly pretended like he was looking for something in his glove compartment. Umber, of course, would never miss an opportunity to be nosy, and he walked right up to his colleague with a smug look on his face.

"Hoy there. Sorry to interrupt. You've got a private office for doing that kind of thing, you know. Unless you're into the whole exhibitionism scene." He waved his hands around in a suggestive fashion on that last part.

Colbert got out of his car. "Not my thing. Just looking for my phone charger."

"Right. Well, if I didn't know better, I'd say you were up to no good out here."

"But you know better, right?"

Umber smiled. He was no fan of Colbert, but he had to tread lightly due to his BFF status with Harmon. "Of course. I'm off to lunch. Ta ta for now."

Seditionists HQ - Los Angeles

"Mr. Johansson?"

Dav hit his intercom irritably as he walked back into his office. "Yes?"

"Mr. Bancroft on the phone for you. Says he's been trying to call your cell."

"Put him through." He looked up at Rupert, who had followed him in after they had just eaten lunch together. "Want to stay, or…"

Rupe wanted to do anything but stay, but his curiosity got the best of him. "Yeah."

"Hey Dav. Did you get my email about the FBI coming to see you and Rupe at 2:30?"

"No, sorry. I've been at lunch."

Hank huffed in annoyance. "If you're going to ignore your cell, at least keep an eye on your damned emails. I've been trying to get a hold of you for an hour."

Daven crooked an eyebrow at Rupert. "I'm sorry, Hank. Rupert is here with me. They're coming at 2:30, you say?"

"Yes. Am I on speaker?"

"Yes."

"Okay. They're going to meet with you first, Rupe. Don't even ask me what the questions are going to be like because I have no idea. It's absolutely imperative that you don't try to act like you're hiding anything."

Rupert glanced at Dav, then back to the phone. "I have nothing to hide, Hank."

"Yeah, I know. But you guys haven't met Salome. If you hesitate on anything, or act like you're trying to spin your answer, she'll pick up on it and start to probe, and it's going to hurt like a son of a bitch. Be honest and candid. Don't fuck around with these guys even in the slightest. Dav, you remember what I told you the other day?"

The receipts. Hank had told him to lie, which was the opposite of what he was saying now. "Yes."

"Good. I'm going to be at the office by 2:30 and we'll talk some more then."

"Hank, why aren't we having our lawyers attend as well?"

Hank cleared his throat. "Yeah, that's the other reason I was calling. I just got off the phone with Brody, and I want him present in everything we do from here on out."

Daven scrunched up his nose. "Brody Camber? He's too young. He's...Hank, he's brand new."

"I agree, Hank," Rupert replied. "He's still got that deer in the headlights look every time someone asks him even the simplest of questions."

"Yeah. He also idolizes us all, and he's hellishly smarter than he looks. Ever had a conversation with him? You'd be surprised how tough it is to keep up."

"Hank-"

"Dav, I've decided on this, and you're not going to change my mind. Everything we say from here on out, he hears. Got it? And don't you dare tell me you're *the one in charge* again."

Rupert looked at Dav in surprise and mouthed, you said *that?* Daven shrugged a little, then turned his attention back to Hank.

"Yes, I hear you. We've got it. See you at 2:30, then?"

"See you then. I'm leaving in just a few." Hank hung up.

"Wow, Dav," Rupert said with a grin. "Way to take the ball and run with it. Was the water in his espresso machine even starting to cool off before you started pulling rank on him?"

Daven ignored him and frowned. "Brody Camber? *Seriously?*"

Hank was of course fully prepared for everyone to be staring at him when he arrived back at the office, but it still threw him off a bit and he felt little more than an exotic animal on display at the zoo as he followed Daven into a conference room.

"I won't lie," Dav said quickly as he shut the door. "Sorry, Hank."

Hank sat down and leaned way back in his chair, crossing his hands over his belly. "Well. You have to, Dav. It's official. I'm fucked."

"What do you mean? What's happened?"

Hank felt strangely calm under the circumstances. "Harmon recorded me in a conversation that can only be construed as blackmail. The FBI has the tape. No jury in their right minds, Urbane or Seditionists, would ever deem it otherwise. I'm looking at five years, minimum, no matter what happens with all the other charges."

Daven was nearly beside himself. "How could you...why would you...Hank, after all the..."

"I know. But what's done is done. So you're going to lie, and you're going to get out of the implication that you fucked around with the news of those receipts in order to avoid alarming our constituents and influencing the vote.”

“That was never my intention!”

Hank huffed. “Fuck your *intention*. It doesn't matter. Perception is reality, and that's what you have to accept. Just like I have. Blackmailing Harmon was never my intention, either. It came out as a sarcastic comment in a moment of anger, yet here I am. Nobody is going to believe that you-”

Daven stood up to cut him off. “No, Hank,” he said firmly. “There’s got to be another way.”

Hank closed his eyes for a long moment. When they reopened, Daven was deeply unsettled by the feeling that a stranger was staring back at him.

“If you don’t lie, I’m going to lose the boys for a minimum of 20 years, because you will *never* be granted custody of them if you throw yourself onto your sword. You take yourself down, you take *them* down, too. Do you understand me, or not? I’m not sure how much clearer I can possibly be.”

Daven shook his head and stared at the floor, unable to accept what he was hearing.

“Dav?” Hank prompted. “You’re *going* to lie, I don't care how much it pains you. Consider it a punishment for fucking up with those receipts. *Then* you're going to take care of my boys and run this organization. That’s what you signed up for the other day, and I expect you to honor that agreement. Are you hearing me at all? Feels like I'm talking to a brick wall."

Daven walked around the conference table in silence, sliding his finger thoughtfully along the back of every chair.

"Need an answer, Dav," Hank said a minute later. "By the way, Stewart and Salome have no idea I'm aware of the tape, so don't mention it."

"What? Then how do you know of it?"

Hank hesitated. "I can't tell you."

Daven threw up his hands in frustration. "For god's sake, Hank. I can't handle all of this right now. You know what? You ask too much of people sometimes. And this is...this is too much."

"I know. I'm sorry for that. But right now, I just need a yes or no answer at the very minimum. Are you going to lie to them, or not?"

The conflicted man in his trademark coat looked away for a minute - which felt like hours to Hank - then finally caught Hank's eye and nodded.

"Thank you," Hank breathed out in relief.

Daven turned and abruptly left the conference room without another word. Hank jumped when the door slammed, but he didn't move to follow his friend. He just sat there, mindlessly twirling his wedding ring around his finger in silence for a full hour, until the expected knock on the door announced the arrival of Stewart and Salome.

CHAPTER SEVEN

Seditionists Headquarters

Wednesday afternoon

"Hey guys," said Hank casually as a file of downturned faces piled into the conference room. "Bringing the whole gang, huh?" He moved aside to make room for Rupert, Daven, Brody, Salome, and Stewart around the table.

Stewart shut the door behind him, but didn't sit down.

"Hello, Hank. Sorry to visit you under these circumstances. Since you're all here and in one room, I wanted to quickly go over what's going to happen on Monday."

"The apocalypse?" Hank joked, not caring about the astonished side glances he received from Rupe and Dav.

Stewart didn't react; he knew Hank well enough to understand that he turned to black humor when he was nervous. "At exactly noon we'll send in an FBI tech to put a special tape across your office door that's illegal to breach. You'll have three hours *after* that to send out a press release, or have a press conference if you prefer, before you need to go to the airport. I would suggest that Daven release an additional statement immediately after your departure."

No one on the room seemed to be breathing all of a sudden, except for Hank.

"Understood. That sounds…very humiliating."

Stewart swallowed hard. "It's not meant to be. You're not going to be dragged out in handcuffs. It's literally just a guy in a suit who will be in and out in five minutes. You'll go to the airport on your own, and travel with whoever you want. We have no intention of turning this into a spectacle."

Hank smiled a little. "Wonderful. I'm looking forward to seeing what the inside of a Philadelphia jail cell looks like. If they're anything like the ones in Los Angeles, I'm in for a fun time. And probably dysentery."

Confusion clouded Stewart's expression at that statement. "Wait, Hank. Back up. We're not locking you up on Monday, for god's sake."

Hank heard Daven and Rupert finally breathe out together. "Oh. I thought…I mean, under arrest usually means 'in jail' to me."

Salome spoke up at this point. "It doesn't for you. You're literally the most famous person in the nation, hardly a flight risk. We'll let you stay in a hotel while the investigation is ongoing."

"I don't want special treatment," Hank lied.

"Trust me, you do. Besides, it's not your decision. I do want to add that before noon Monday, your organization is to maintain your silence and not speak to the media or make any statements." She looked around the room. "Mr. Johansson, Mr. Aster, any questions?"

Daven looked at Hank, but there was hardly any recognition in the glance. Dav was like a man defeated, and Hank knew it was because the lie had been told. He was profoundly relieved, no matter how much his friend hated him for it.

Rupert asked carefully, "When will the FBI be releasing details of the charges to the public?"

Salome replied, "That's something I need to discuss with Hank. He will have a lot of control over what gets said on Monday, depending on how he wishes to proceed. However, the FBI will craft the statement, not the Seditionists or the Urbanes. We have no intention of enabling any more public slap fights between your parties."

"Right," Rupert replied in obvious disappointment. "So you're saying that absolutely nothing is up to us from this point on, as far as PR goes."

"Untrue. Stewart just told you you'll have time to make a statement or a press conference between noon and three on Monday."

"Yeah, but that's after the fact. What about before? Excuse me for not appreciating the fact that we basically have to sit on our hands and let the rumors get out of hand while you two get to sit back and enjoy the show."

Hank snapped out of his reverie at the remark as Salome bristled.

"Rupe," he chided warningly. "Let it go. We'll talk later."

"Seriously, Hank? No. It's bullshit. You should see what the news is already saying. Which, by the way, I blame the FBI for." He turned to Stewart. "Why did you let this get leaked?"

"Rupe, if you don't shut up-" Hank began, but Salome held a hand up and everyone instantly settled down and fell quiet again.

"It's alright, Hank. I'll answer that. The Urbanes leaked it, not us. They have been reprimanded for it already."

Daven looked at Hank and scoffed. "Harmon wouldn't have done that," he muttered. "Not while he's barely holding on to his job."

"Colbert all the way," Hank agreed bitterly.

"Umber," put in Rupert sullenly. "Wolf in sheep's clothing, that one."

"But smarter than Harmon and Colbert put together, and that's not saying much," Hank refuted hotly.

"Let's settle down, please," Salome said firmly. The room went silent again. "If there are no further questions or arguments, we should move forward."

"No," replied Dav.

"This is bullshit," muttered Rupe under his breath.

"*Rupert*," Hank growled.

"No questions, Ms. Danby," Rupert amended politely, finally accepting that he was pushing Hank too far.

She nodded. "That will be all then. We'll be in touch again soon."

The door shut behind the two men as they left, and Hank looked at Brody for the first time. "You doing okay?"

"Yes, sir," the young man answered confidently.

"Do you wish to speak with me alone before we get started?"

"No, sir. But you need to tell me if you're uncomfortable answering a question *before* you answer it, not afterwards. I will ask for clarification, or have it rephrased or removed from the record. Don't say anything ambiguous, try to stick to yes and no and short explanations. Understood?"

"Yes, sir." He smiled wryly, idly wondering at the same time if Brody had also spoken to Dav and Rupe in such an authoritative manner. He could imagine both men being deeply offended by such unexpected sassiness from the new guy, and the thought amused him for a few precious moments.

Stewart opened his binder and picked up a pen. "Let's start with the subpoena. I had to rewrite it on the way to Los Angeles to include some revisions from Harmon. The very first thing I want to ask you is extraordinarily delicate, to say the least, and your answer could determine if there will be additional charges."

"Way to jump right in," Hank mused bitterly. "Not even a softball question first, huh? By the way, please accept my apologies for Rupert's behavior. I'll be having a word with him later."

"It's alright, Hank. He was fine in the interview, and he's not exactly wrong about his concerns. I'll revisit that issue with the president and see what he says."

"Thank you."

Stewart looked down at his notes, obviously feeling uncomfortable about the incident nonetheless. "Moving on. Harmon wants to lay additional charges of unlawful corporate espionage because he has evidence that one of your informants took copies of proprietary documents at your direction. If you're aware of any such actions, you need to tell me now. If we find out later, things are going to get ugly very quickly."

Fuck. Hank cleared his throat. "I know of one such action. One of my informants tried to bring me a copy of an Urbane's legal document on his own accord. I was incensed, to say the least, and made him shred it on the spot. I never laid a single finger on it, nor did I ask for anything like that to be taken."

Salome was stone-faced. "What kind of document?"

Fuck, again. "A draft of the original lawsuit complaint."

Stewart's jaw dropped. "That's...okay, that's a felony offense on its own."

"I'm not telling you who it was, so don't ask," Hank bristled.

Brody leaned over to his new boss and said quietly, "You don't have to tell them. Stay calm."

Hank took a deep breath and tried again to answer Stewart more diplomatically. "Yes. I'm aware it was against the law. That's why I ordered it shredded immediately, in front of the group, so that four people could witness it. I never touched it."

Salome set down her pen and picked up a bottle of water. "Was this person searched for additional copies of the document, including his belongings?"

"Yes. None were found." That was the truth, technically. The secret copy had not been found when Pamela searched the briefcase.

Salome and Stewart exchanged glances, and Hank suddenly became deeply uncomfortable. He hadn't yet shredded the second copy; it was in a locked drawer in his desk at home. He vowed to immediately shred it after reading it once more, the moment he got home.

"Right, so..." Salome took a deep breath and drank some more water. "This is a problem, Hank. If I had your offices searched right now, would we find any other illicit documents?"

"I believe a warrant is required to search my offices. Is that correct, Brody?"

"Yes, sir."

"We're not searching anything," Salome clarified irritably. "I'm asking you a question, and I expect you to answer it."

Stewart caught the momentary flash in Hank's eye that indicated he was about to lie. Something he had never seen before in him, but had seen a thousand times before in other people. It was unmistakable.

"No. You won't find anything," Hank said steadily.

"Thank you. Moving on-" she stopped herself as her phone rang. "I'm very sorry, gentlemen, this is the president. I have to take it. Please excuse me."

She got up and disappeared into the private washroom that was connected to the conference room.

Stewart cleared his throat roughly and looked at the lawyer. "Mr. Camber, with Hank's permission will you please leave us alone for a moment? Thanks."

Hank nodded, and the young man left. Stewart looked Hank right in the eyes and didn't waver. "You're lying, Hank. Stop it, or I will seal up both your offices within the hour and you'll never get the chance to go back in. Do you understand me?"

Hank shifted uncomfortably in his chair. "Do it, then, if you're so convinced."

"You also told Daven to lie. Tell the truth from this point on, or I'll do it for you. We clear?"

Hank picked at a piece of loose laquer on the table and smirked. "Just from this point on, huh?"

Stewart sighed and shook his head. "Jesus Christ, Hank. You've really…I don't even know what to say. Get your lawyer back in here, please, before I say something I'll regret."

"Like what? What else could you possibly do to dig my grave any deeper?"

"You're trying to blame this on me? Unbelievable! I'm trying to help you, you stubborn fucker," Stewart hissed.

"I appreciate the support," Hank replied insincerely.

"Support that's *always* been there, by the way, if you'd ever take a moment to realize it. Haven't you ever noticed that everyone is on your side, except you? Even Harmon, for god's sake."

Hank sat up straighter. "Even Harmon? What the hell does *that* mean?"

"Forget it. I need to stop talking." Stewart got up and pulled open the door to let Brody back in before either of them could say anything else.

Hank just sat there in silence, feeling like he had received several gut punches in a row.

Your transparency will be the death of you.

I'm trying to help you, you stubborn fucker.

Everyone is on your side, except you.

Even Harmon.

"Well, that was fun," Hank said blandly as he strolled into Daven's office two hours after he had last seen him. Rupert was there, too, looking just as depressed as Hank felt.

Dav stood up. "What happened? Everything okay?"

"Ha. When was the last time anything was okay around here?"

"What's going to happen now?" asked Rupert with deep concern. "And please, no more joking."

"Well...I have four days to mount my defense for the charges that are coming on Monday. Blackmail, espionage, bribery, et cetera." He held up the subpoena. "It's all in here. The worst part is something I need to discuss with Daven alone, since it

95

concerns the boys. Not that I don't want you in on the discussion, Rupe, but it truly doesn't make sense to-"

"It's alright," Rupert replied quickly. "I understand. You two definitely need to talk."

"Wait, let's not jump ahead," Daven insisted. "Besides the tape, Hank, what else do they have on you?"

"What tape?" Rupe asked, puzzled.

Hank rubbed his temples. "Guys, I...there's so much I need to tell you. Let's meet in the morning, okay? Clear your calendars. I've got to go home."

Hank didn't show up for the meeting on Thursday morning, so around 10am Daven took a car to the house to check on him. He already knew he was okay - as in alive and acting normally - because he had spoken to Avery already once he had gotten too concerned to wait any longer.

He was shocked to the core when the guard at the gate turned him away.

"Mr. Bancroft doesn't wish to have any visitors right now. Sorry, sir," said a clearly embarrassed Martinez.

"I...but...does he know it's me?"

"Yes, sir. Just spoke to him. He said to deny you entry."

You've got to be kidding me, Dav thought, stunned beyond description.

"Very well, I...thank you?"

He went back to the office and continued reading through all of Hank's old emails to find any way out of this mess. Again. Around 4pm, Rupert all but burst through the door.

"Dav! Turn on the news!" He ran to the television and quickly found the right channel, and Daven watched in stony, shocked silence as Hank appeared, walking confidently down the stairs of a private plane.

- arrived approximately half an hour ago at the private airstrip in New Castle, about 35 miles outside of Philadelphia. He was taken into custody by Salome Danby on the tarmac and is presumably being driven to FBI headquarters. A spokesperson for the FBI has stated that a statement will be released in two hours. As the story develops we will continue to update you.

The shot changed to a blurry aerial view of the town car, not moving in the standstill traffic on 95.

Daven couldn't breathe, or speak. He was vaguely aware of his cell phone ringing in his pocket, and strictly by force of habit he pulled it out mechanically and flipped it open.

It was pretty much the last person he could imagine having anything coherent to say to at the moment.

"Hello, Floyd."

"Uncle Dav? I'm sorry to bother you. When are you going to be home? I'm kind of freaking out."

Daven's chest tightened. "Right now, Floyd. I'm coming. Hold on."

CHAPTER EIGHT

Daven realized on the way to the Bancroft house that Floyd would probably be on the floor in a fit of hyperventilation when he arrived, but he didn't have the name or number to the boy's doctor, nor any idea of if or when she needed to be called. It didn't occur to him, though, that there were 17 other people in the household - plus Theo - who already had this information. He was used to living completely alone, so the thought of 20 people living under one roof, and who all looked out for each other, was completely foreign to him.

Therefore, when the gates to the estate opened up immediately upon the arrival of his town car (the guard didn't even bother to come out of the booth) he raced up to the front door with an oppressive feeling of barely controlled panic. Just like Floyd was feeling right now, he figured.

Brittany opened the door for him with a small smile, and Daven was surprised to find Floyd and Theo merely sitting on the couch, chatting and eating Cheez-Its like nothing was wrong. He hesitated, then went and sat down beside them, dreading what he was about to hear next.

"Hello, boys. How are you doing?"

"Not so good. Dad's not coming back," Theo blurted casually. "Want some Cheez-Its?"

Daven paused, shook his head, and studied Floyd's calm expression in deep confusion. "Floyd, I thought...you said you were freaking out, so I raced here as fast as I could. What's going on?"

"He wasn't freaking out," Theo answered with a mouthful of crackers. "He's fine!"

Floyd flipped to the next page of his comic book. "Yeah, I'm fine, Uncle Dav. We just got home from school. But dad's in Philadelphia for a little while, so he wants you to stay with us."

"Forever," interjected Theo with all the sullen attitude that only 12-year old boys were capable of.

"Maybe. Is that why you're home early?" Floyd asked offhandedly.

"I...sure. Yes." Daven turned to look helplessly at Brittany, whose expression offered no further clues. He turned back to the boys again. "When I find out what your dad is up to, I'll let you know. In the meantime-"

Floyd answered, "It's okay, we already know. He left you a note in the study with the rules we have to follow and stuff until he gets back." Floyd stood up and set down the box of Cheez-Its. "I'll show you where it is. Want something to drink first?"

"No, thanks."

Daven followed the teenager in wonder, feeling like he was in the Twilight Zone.

Until they arrived in the study, that is. It turned out Floyd had just been staying strong and unconcerned for Theo's sake; once the door shut and he was alone with his "uncle," he completely lost it. Daven grabbed the box of Kleenex and caught Floyd just as the boy collapsed onto the couch and all but melted into him in tearful anguish.

After half an hour of calming Floyd, who thankfully didn't have a full-fledged panic attack, Daven slowly peeled himself off the couch and moved towards the manila envelope on the desk. It contained just a few sheets of paper topped by a handwritten letter on Hank's personal letterhead.

Floyd looked up at him questioningly from where he was lying listlessly, so Daven felt compelled to explain. "I don't think your dad meant for you to see this, based on the way it's sealed. I'm going to read it to myself first, okay? And I'll share with you what I can."

He only got a bare nod of a response, but that was enough, and he tore open the flap in fretful anticipation.

Dav - I left early for Philadelphia to make sure there was enough time to wrap this thing up before March 31. Enclosed is a list of all the standing rules I have for my sons. Floyd will follow them except for the one about not watching the news, so I've had all the televisions removed and locked in basement storage, except for the one in my bedroom sitting room, which is off-limits to the boys at all times. The door's passcode is 1182. Theo is pretty good on the whole, but watch his sugar intake carefully or he'll be bouncing off the walls 24 hours a day.

Also enclosed is a list of usernames and password for all of my online accounts, as well as the combination code to my safe. In there, you'll find more information which you can access on April 1 if I haven't returned by then. As for the investigation, you and Rupert are to stay out of it completely from now on unless you are asked specifically for information by the FBI. There's nothing else you can do at this point. Go back to work as usual and be the amazing leader that I know you are (need to work on your people skills, though...they're a little rusty.) I'll be in touch as soon as I can. Stay true. -Hank

Daven read it four times, his heart falling further and further into the abyss each time - then looked across at Floyd, who had sat up and was fully alert again.

"What did your dad tell you?" he croaked. "Try to remember exactly."

"Yes, sir."

"Don't call me sir."

"Sorry. Dad said he...he..."

Daven set the letter down and crossed back to Floyd, taking the chair directly across from him. "I know this is hard, but you have to tell me. I didn't have time to talk to him before he left, and his trip was a complete surprise to me."

Floyd nodded again, then wiped his eyes for the hundredth time. "Last night when he got home from work, he said he was going to be gone for a while. Like, maybe years. We..."

"Be strong, Floyd. Continue."

"Sorry, I'm trying. He said a lot, I don't remember it all. But I understand what's going on. He's going to Philadelphia to try to get exhilarated."

"Exonerated," Dav correctly, much less gently than he intended.

"Exonerated. But he doesn't know if he can. He doesn't think he can. He said...he'll probably be back before I graduate college."

Daven stood up, unable to bear another moment of sitting still. This was a bloody disaster.

"I don't really know what else to say, Uncle Dav," Floyd continued, fearing that the man was annoyed at him, rather than at his father. "We spent all our time since then just being together, and saying goodbye, but he still made us go to school this morning after he left for the airport."

That sounded just like Hank; as hardass as ever even under the most dire circumstances. "How is Theo doing?"

Floyd shrugged. "Fine. I don't think it's hit him yet. Anyway, then dad told me to call you at four o'clock because you'd know by then that he was in Philadelphia."

Daven nodded. "Anything else you need to tell me?"

"Not really. Not work related, anyway. He told us we had to listen to you and not give you a hard time. Which we won't, Uncle Dav, I swear."

"I know. Floyd, you look pale. Why don't you go lay down for a little bit in your room? I'll meet you there in a few minutes. Can you grab me something to drink? I don't care what. I need to call Rupert to let him know you're okay, and then I'll be right there."

"Okay. Can I take the dogs up with me?"

Daven hesitated. "What would your dad say to that?"

"He'd...." Floyd hesitated. "He'd say no. They aren't allowed on the second floor."

"Then no. Go on, I'll see you in a minute."

Floyd pulled himself up with a grumble and left, and Daven dialed his friend as fast as he could manage. Rupe picked up halfway through the first ring, his tone angry and hurried.

"What the fuck is going on, Dav? You disappeared on me and I've been dealing with a fucking five-alarm fire here without any kind of guidance or information. Thanks a lot for just bailing out and leaving me a hell of a mess to clean up."

"Calm down. I had to tend to Floyd. Turns out Hank left me a letter." Daven read the most relevant parts to him and was met with a deafening silence on the other end of the line.

"Rupe..?"

"Yeah. I'm here. What the fuck are we supposed to tell our constituents? Never mind them, what about our own employees? Not to mention the media. God damn it, Hank."

Daven put the letter into a drawer that had the key in the lock, then removed the key and put it into his pocket. "First of all, stop cussing at me. It's not helping. Secondly, don't worry about the media. We're under a gag order so they don't matter at the moment. Send out a company-wide email to let our employees know we'll have an all-hands meeting tomorrow at 10am."

"What are you going to say?"

"I have no idea yet. I'll call you back in an hour."

He almost put the phone back in his pocket, but changed his mind and left it on the desk. There were well over 50 missed calls already, and the buzzing reminders were annoying him. Theo wasn't in the living room when he passed through, so he went straight to Floyd's room and shut the door behind him. Then he pulled up a desk chair next to the bed. Floyd was facing the wall and under all his sheets and blankets.

"There's a root beer for you on my nightstand," he mumbled, and Dav reached over and took it gratefully.

"Thanks. Are you alright?"

"Yeah. Sleepy. I was up all night."

"Okay. Do you need anything?"

Floyd didn't say anything at first, but then he flipped onto his back and stared at the ceiling. "I got in trouble with Mrs. Aster today."

"For what?" Daven asked with a slight choking reaction; he was so *not* ready to be a father and this kind of talk made him extremely nervous.

"I wasn't very nice to her."

"Okay. You want me to talk to her and explain?"

"Yeah. Please."

Daven nodded. "Consider it done. Don't worry about it. You were under a lot of stress today."

"Uncle Dav?" Floyd said after a long moment of silence.

"Yes?"

"I think I'm going to throw up."

Me too, thought Daven as he reached behind him for the trash can.

9 781801 934763